John Hall-Stevenson

Moral Tales: A Christmas night's entertainment

A Christmas Night's Entertainment

John Hall-Stevenson

Moral Tales: A Christmas night's entertainment
A Christmas Night's Entertainment

ISBN/EAN: 9783743386624

Manufactured in Europe, USA, Canada, Australia, Japa

Cover: Foto ©Andreas Hilbeck / pixelio.de

Manufactured and distributed by brebook publishing software
(www.brebook.com)

John Hall-Stevenson

Moral Tales: A Christmas night's entertainment

MORAL TALES,

A

CHRISTMAS NIGHT'S

ENTERTAINMENT.

BY LADY ✶✶✶✶✶✶.

A NEW EDITION.

LONDON:

PRINTED FOR T. BECKET, PALL-MALL. MDCCLXXXIII.

[PRICE HALF A CROWN.]

ADVERTISEMENT.

A Certain Lady of Fashion, in the Christmas Holidays, formed a Belle Assemblée at the Seat of her Ancestors. On one of those Days, in passing with her Company to the Eating-Room, through the venerable old Hall, she observed,

’Twas merry in the Hall,
When Beards wagg’d all.

You are not, said she, to imagine that there were no Ladies there; but whilst our Grandsires were busy with their Beards, our Grandmothers were as busy with their tongues. Besides, *Animal sans Barbe*, does not enter into the definition of our Sex; neither is a Beard any essential Distinction; there are whole Nations of Men that have none at all.

There were no Card-tables in those merry Days, no *Trouble—Fete-politicks*; no *Seccatori*, or Professors of small Talk. Pray let us make a Trial, after Supper, of the Christmas Festivities of those happy Times. There shall be a round Table, with the Ingredients for Mirth and Jollity, and we will meet here and sit round about our Coal Fire.

At the Time appointed, the Lady of the House presented a Pair of China Basons, one for the Ladies, the other for the Gentlemen, with Tickets, inscribed with the Names and Characters they were to take and personate for the Night; the Hostess only excepted, who was to set off with a merry Tale, and to call upon the whole Company successively, for one of the same fashion. The effect of the Lottery may be conceived ccived by the Examples following: The Parfon's Wife was drawn by a Countefs; the Parfon, by an Alderman of London; the Baronefs, by a celebrated Actrefs; the Baron, by a little good natured witty Dramatift; the Lawyer, by a Right Honourable Captain of a Man of War; the Phyfician, by a fprightly Officer, his *prochain Ami*; and the Apothecay, by a Welch Judge.

The Lady of the Houfe prefaced her Tale by obferving, that Squeamifhnefs, Prudery, and Affectation, were always banifhed upon fuch Occafions; and that in the narrative Style, they muft conform, and fhe would give them an Example, to the old Style of Chriftmas, and ufe the Licence of the Seafon. Right, faid the Parfon; and as to you, Gentlemen, (I fpeak to every Individual)

—— Age, Libertate, Decembri,
Quando ita Majores voluere, Utere, Narra.

LATELY PUBLISHED,

1. CRAZY TALES. In a neat Pocket Volume. Price 2s. 6d.

2. THE SAME BOOK, WITH FABLES FOR GROWN GENTLEMEN;

And a FRONTISPIECE, reprefenting CRAZY-CASTLE. In a large Size. Price 4s. fewed.

MORAL TALES.

MY LADY'S TALE.

TALE I.

RASH, poor, and ever in a hurry,
    'Till he was far advanc'd in age,
A certain General like * * * * * *,
    At laſt grew cautious, rich, and ſage :
With all the ſubſidies of life,
    All but an heir and a young lively wife ;
    Young ſhe muſt be, for reaſons good,
      Not to excite paſſionate dealings,
To keep him warm with her warm blood,
      And to indulge his ſober feelings :
    The wife he got, but left the care
    To Providence and her, to make his heir.

At

At firſt a blaze, or two at moſt

  Appear'd, juſt like a fire of ſtubble,

That cannot either bake or roaſt,

  Or broil, or make the kettle bubble;

 But ſeldom, after that auſpicious day,

 The noble General fired, except in play.

One night he gave a falſe alarm,

  Which ſhe moſt patiently endur'd,

I thank my ſtars there is no harm,

  She whiſper'd to herſelf, inſur'd,*

 Howe'er, to cover his diſgrace,

 She let him keep manœuvring round the place.

His nightly fondling and ſtroking,

  She bore with reſignation meek;

When he became downright provoking,

  She made him quiet for a week.

 It was not oft, you underſtand,

 That ſhe was forc'd to take the taſk in hand.

'Tir'd of his motions and parading,

  To drop all metaphors of war,

She made him ſtick to ſerenading,

  To twang and finger her guitar,

 Like a child's fiddle, to divert young chicks,

 From clamb'ring up and playing naughty tricks.

* Metaphor taken from a policy of inſurance againſt fire, for a trifling conſideration.

By

By independence held out to his dear,
　　By a fincere emancipation,
He gain'd, like Fox, peace and good cheer,
　　Befides a helping hand upon occafion :
　　As to their love, content with thefe conceffions,
　　They left their jewels to their own difcretions.
The General thus addrefs'd the Fair,
　　Toffing and tumbling in her neft :
Get me a Deputy, indeed a pair,
　　For fear of accidents, is beft :
　　But firft, confult your wife, experienc'd dam,
　　Truft her judicious eye, my tender lamb.
He might have fpar'd his curtain lecture,
　　His tender lamb, for all her youth,
Was never guided by conjecture,
　　Or meer appearances of truth :
　　Neither confenting nor denying,
　　She took no meafures without trying.
So by repeated trials, in the end,
　　And wifely taking nought for granted,
She found the fteady friend,
　　And deputy, the General wanted.
In fine, without more fufs or teafing,
　　She made her choice, and chofe difcreetly :
The ftream of time flow'd fmooth and pleafing,
　　Not only pleafingly, but fweetly ;

So much, that the whole veteran corps,

    Envied the General more and more.

Replete with gratitude, the Dame,

    Yielded to all his weakeſt fancies ;

And by a bluſh of ſimpering ſhame,

    Vouch'd for his feats, and conjugal romances.

All which, as I before related,

    Made the old General envied, if not hated.

Young folks are apt, in many a caſe,

    Left to themſelves, without a warden,

To diſregard both time and place,

    Like Eve and Adam in the garden.

They take a turn, they look about,

    And ſeeing nought to fear, conceive no doubt ;

Taking their paſtime in an arbour,

    Our friends were by the Chaplain ſpied,

Like frigates riding in an harbour,

    With their ſails furl'd, in naked pride :

The Prieſt, like Satan, ſigh'd, and ſaw with ſpite,

Adam and Eve in primitive delight.

Before they reach'd the bower of bliſs,

    At the firſt glance, you may ſuppoſe,

Down dropp'd the Prieſt, ſquat like a miſs,

    Stepping aſide to pluck a roſe.

Cowering he watch'd, amidſt the ſhrubs hard by

A… envious toad, like Milton's wicked ſpy.

                          When

When the fcene clos'd, the fpy withdrew,
　　With marks of grief and indignation,
Revealing every thing he knew
　　Relating to the incarnation.
Lock'd in each others arms they play'd,
　　Faften'd and glew'd from head to foot,
The pair conjoin'd, you would have faid,
　　Were grown together like a double nut.
　Their fprings and movements equal and exact,
　As if they were but one in fact.
　The General fmil'd, and heard the Doctor's tattle,
　Calm and ferene, as in a field of battle.
'Twas a fine fight, I envy you the pleafure;
　　I know, faid he, your hate to blabs and praters,
And am rejoic'd, and happy beyond meafure,
　　That none but God and you were the fpectators.
Depend upon't fhe fhall be told,
　　When fhe's difpos'd to go fo light and thin;
To run no more fuch rifks of catching cold,
　　But take her exercife within.
I love my wife, I feel her merits,
　　I am her doctor, and advife,
For her hyftericks, and low fpirits
　　This brifk de-obftruent exercife.

C

A hundred pounds a year I pay her fquire,
 I feed him fumptuoufly, and therewithal
The labourer is worthy of his hire,
 And always ready at a call.
 Know you, the General faid to the Divine,
 A General's lady better off than mine?
 The Prieft reply'd, and anfwer'd well,
 Sir, if I knew, I would not tell.
I could name one, one every way,
 As capable, as brifk and ftout,
A much more proper *Cicefbi*
 Either within doors, or without;
 And one he faid, cocking his thumb,
That would have done the job for half the fum.

THE MORAL, BY THE DRAMATIST.

 All tales and fables, long or fhort,
  Æfop's or Homer's, feign'd or true,
Muft have a moral of fome fort,
  For our inftruction, fays Boffu.
We learn this truth from Homer's fongs,
  When youth and infolence confpire,
Grievous diffenfions and great wrongs,
  Arife from paffion fet on fire.

His

His tale is founded upon anger,
    With anger's terrible effects ;
This upon impotence and languor,
    With age's rifible defects.

They both agree in one conclufion,
    Where there's no harmony all is confufion ;
In ftates, in fenates, camps and fleets,
And now and then in wedding fheets.

If an old fellow goes to bed
    With his young bride, and gets next morn,
Inftead of his bride's maidenhead,
    The maiden-bride's contempt and fcorn ;
The fureft way to fet things right,
    And to do juftice to the bride,
Is to get up and take his flight,
    Or take her General for his guide :
Who fail'd through time with a fine breeze,
    Through pleafant days and nights of eafe :
For the connubial clog and yoke,
    Heavy to me, not light to you,
To him was a meer joke,
    Eafy it fat like an old fhoe.

THE

THE PARSON'S WIFE.

TALE II.

SUE, and another country lafs,
  With ploughman Dick, a gibing knave,
Were at the wedding of an afs,
    And all of them look'd very grave.
The marriage ceremony done ;
    The laffes cried, Dick, fhew your fkill,
If you are for a bit of fun,
    Chufe one of us, take which you will.
Richard malicioufly reply'd,
    Thinking to difconcert the jades,
Faith I would rather take the bride,
    If I might chufe, than her bride-maids.
I do believe you, Dick, faid Sue,
    And jogg'd her partner, with a grin :
We would take Jack rather than you,
    If 'twas not for the fin.

MORAL.

This is not an immoral Tale,
    The Parfon to his praife and glory,
Exhibited over his ale,
    A moral to his Spoufe's ftory.

If

If Mofes had not been fo clear
    And circumftantial in God's orders,
The carnal appetites, I fear,
    Would often get beyond the borders;
    There would be many a ftrange wedding,
    Some without either bed or bedding.
If the Divine Legation had not fhewn it,
    How fhould unletter'd people know,
    Whether it was a fin or no?
Even Warburton would not have known it.
And therefore, as I faid above,
    Mofes was told to teach the Jews,
How and with whom they might make love:
    God would not let them pick and chufe.
His chofen people all their lives,
    Lov'd novelties, as they do now;
God knew that they would leave their wives
    At any time to kifs a cow.
The Jewifh ladies were like ours,
    Fickle, not nice in their amours:
And if it had not been forbid,
    Many might have been got with kid.

D

THE

THE PARSON'S TALE.

SEEING IS BELIEVING.

TALE III.

THOMAS came running to the mill,
    As Will was ftanding at the door,
Would you believe it, neighbour Will?
    Said Tom, my wife's an errant whore.
With colours flying, drums a pair,
    I left her very hard at work,
Toffing the Squire up in the air,
    As if he had been made of cork.
You know the burthen is not light,
    He was not born to be a jockey,
And to add fomething to the weight,
    His Worfhip was a little rocky.
From my relation I prefume,
    Neighbour, you will conclude and gather,
That he was in a plaguy fume,
    And fhe all over in a lather.
I never thought, as I'm a finner,
    That Moll had any fporting blood,
Or any kind of mettle in her,
    No more than in a log of wood.

At

At any moment of a day,
　　My wife faid, Will takes as much pains:
I make her pockets ring and play,
　　Jingling her keys about like chains.
And yet no fempftrefs with a thimble,
　　That fits all day upon her crupper,
Can be more mettlefome and nimble,
　　Or readier for it, after fupper.
Where did you leave your wife? faid he——
　　Behind yon' ftack, where fhe lies dry,
Run and peep through the hedge and fee,
　　Said Tom, if fhe begin to fly.
　Will ran and peep'd, and then crept nigher,
　And then cried, Thomas, you're a lyar.
I fee them at it, and fee clear,
　　'Tis not your Moll, but my fweet Nell;
The devil, I hope, that brought her here,
　　Will carry her back with him to hell.
I knew, and would have laid my life,
　　Said Will, if I had bid you go,
To fee the paftime of your wife,
　　You would not run to fee the fhew;
　But you would fcamper to the ftack,
　To fee my wife upon her back.

The

The only way that I would act,
    The only way I would advise,
And the beft way to prove the fact,
    Is to appeal to your own eyes.

M O R A L.

Segnius irritant animos dimiffa per anrem,
    Quam quæ funt oculis fubjecta fidelibus, & quæ
Ipfe fibi tradit fpectator.————

An offer from one, of feventy-four,
    Was grateful to the royal hearing,
If one-by-felf-one had offer'd one more,
    Keppel would think that one was jeering.
The offer might furprife a tar,
    The Lawyer cried, taking off Lee:
To fee the L——r man of war,
    I do confefs would furprife me.——
    There is fome difference faid the fcoffer,
    Between an offering and an offer;
    Sam offer'd Jack a horfe---where is he Sam?
    Sam anfwer'd, in the matrix of his dar..
Where are my fhips, cried Lewis, feize,
    That many a town and province offers?
Sire, faid the daughter of Therefe,
    Breeding like Spider's eggs, in empty coffers.

T H E

THE ASSOCIATION.

THE SQUIRE'S TALE.

TALE IV.

A Village Burgher, was Ralph Crop,.
    A grocer without guile or malice;
The mafter of the grocer's fhop,
    And of Ralph Crop, was Miftrefs Alice.
When Alice was engag'd, her damfel Kate,
    When Ralph her fpoufe was abfent too,
Did quite as well, for fhe could fell and prate,
    Better, perhaps, than Crop could do.
Crop was juft gone to market-town,
    And all the world was there---'twas the fair day,---
To buy his wife a cap and gown,
    To fhew his tafte, and make her fhew away.
All the world knows, that certain glances,
    Interpret certain women's fancies.
The Excifeman was a fine obferver,
    And faw from Alice's black eyes,
That all the world could not preferve her,
    From being taken by furprife.

E

Treading the fhop, he caft the dye,

  He pafs'd the Rubicon and met her ;

And in the twinkling of an eye,

  Carry'd his point, and overfet her.

He pafs'd the Rubicon, it means in verfe,

He was not bafhful for her looking fierce :

At the firft onfet, Myles averr'd,

He took the Lion by the beard.

For Hercules, without a fcratch or rúb,

  Taking poffeffion of that feature,

With his great club,

  Terrify'd and fubdu'd the creature.

Myles having conquer'd her difdain,

  (Alice and Myles were in their prime,)

They did not fpend their hours in vain,

  But made the propereft ufe of time.

Ralph was returning with his fairing,

  And at the door, juft after pairing.

Neither fufpecting any harm,

  Behold Crop enters with his riches,

A gown and cap under his arm, .

  As Myles was pulling up his breeches.---

I am glad you left the fair fo foon,

  His wife cry'd out---the Excifeman there,

Whipt in juft now, this afternoón,

  Stark ftaring mad as a March hare,

Had he not known you by your blowing,
	Had not he heard you at the door,
That very moment he was going
	To f--t upon the parlour floor ;
And fwore, that if I call'd or ftir'd,
	The brute would make me eat his---merde.
What did you mean, faid Crop, by this ?
	Nothing at all, faid Myles, amifs.
Behold faid one, that fhall be namelefs,
	Before her window, Miftrefs Blamelefs ;
Poor foul, fhe looks quite melancholy,
	Try Myles, fome heads were made for horns.
To try, faid I, would be a monftrous folly,
	Try to lick honey off the thorns ;
Even fuppofe what cannot be fuppofed,
	I would not wrong a friend, fo well difpofed ;
I'll put as hard a cafe, I think,
	A rump and dozen---let us wager,
I'll make no love, but make a ftink,
	Shall cure her vapours, I'll engage her.
Mind ; I'll untrufs down to the feet,
	And do my n---s before her face,
Plump on the floor, and for my treat,
	She fhall be thankful and fay grace.
If you had not ftept in between,
	I fhould have won the wager clean :

Nothing

Nothing amifs was meant, I knew,

My friend here, loved a harmlefs joke,

The thought was comical and new,

'Twould make him laugh ready to choak.

Marry come up, my dirty Coufin,

Said Alice, with your rump and dozen ;

Laugh ! laugh at what, you filthy beaft ?

If he had laugh'd at fuch a thing,

I would have made both his ears ring ;

For one whole fortnight at the leaft.

Go, pay the wager you have loft ;

I'm glad, faid Crop, that he was taken in,

A rump and dozen's no fmall coft,

And as to laughing, let them laugh that win.

M O R A L

A cafe in point, faid fly Sir John,

To prove two heads better than one.

One gives a hint, and only moves it,

The fecond takes it, and improves it ?

I grant your maxim, faid his Dame,

If both their interefts are the fame.

The Baron cried, the moral's fine,

I fmoke two rogues, and one defign.

I fee

I fee too rogues together pull,
 Two patriots fet out together,
 In dirty roads and in foul weather,
To make a fool of poor John Bull.

HOB IN THE WELL.

SIR JOHN'S TALE.

TALE V.

A Taylor, bodkin-ftitch, in a few years,
 Grew rich, and is encreafing ftill,
By the nice conduct of his fheers,
 And fkill in drawing up a bill.
A bill, like any bill of Chancery,
 Or my Lord North's bill of Fine---anfery---
His Budget like a giblet pie,
 Furnifh'd with gizzards, hearts and liver,
 Pinions, necks, feet, and blood for ever,
And goofe-cap heads that once look'd high.
 Twelve miles from York, or thereabout,
 Stitch bought a farm, he call'd Surtout——
His agent, every week that came,
 Was fure to fend him a ftout hare,
Pigeons, and now and then fome game,
 With rabbits, taken in a fnare.

F

In fine, Stitch liv'd like any Lord,

 Any Lord Mayor, that draws long corks---

Turkeys and geefe fmoak'd on his board,

 Like geefe upon his board of works.

 Befides, his farm produc'd him clear

 In cafh two hundred pounds a year.

Robin, a farmer, was his factor,

 The taylor would not part with Hob,

So good a factor and tranfactor,

 For the beft regimental job ;

Not to take meafure of the King,

 Although, perhaps, by fuch an honour,

His wife, a proud difdainful thing,

 Might not take quite fo much upon her :

 A Knight's third coufin, where's the wonder

 If Bodkin truckl'd and knock'd under ?

Obferve, that every Eafter Sunday,

 Hob came to feaft on pafchal lamb,

And then return'd on Eafter Monday

 To Tanfy pudding and a ham.

The beds were full, when Robin came,

 As harmlefs as his namefake bird,

 Robin was forc'd to make a third,

And pig with Bodkin and his Dame.

Hob

Hob in his breeches went to bed,
    And Miftrefs Stitch was in the middle,
Her face turn'd clofe to Bodkin's head,
    To leather breeches her bum-fiddle.
  Bodkin's horn foon began to blow,
  Hob was awake, and fhe alfo.
On certain fignals from behind,
    Hob his mafk'd battery difclos'd,
Summon'd the fort, which was refign'd
    Upon the terms that he propos'd.
They were oblig'd to take their leave
    At laft for fear of a furprize,
Not without tears, you may believe,
    And fleep in earneft clos'd their eyes.
Recruited with a four hours nap,
    Hob gave her notice of his rifing,
Firft at the door he gave a tap,
    And then a rap that was furprifing:
As Madam Stitch in the conclufion,
    Receiv'd the *coup-de-grace* and was expiring.
Bodkin was wak'd by a contufion,
    Studied the point and could not help admiring;
And then put back his hand, and lo!
He found Hob in the well below.
Steal off, faid Stitch, and quit your ground,
'Tis well for you fhe fleeps fo found.

If

If my wife wakes and finds you got
  Out of your road, into her quarters,
She'll scratch your eyes out, she's so hot,
  And strangle you in her Bath garters.
 When I got there, said Hob, or how,
 I know no more than you, I vow;
But in the well have got through thick and thin---
  Oft in my sleep I walk, they say,
And in my sleep must have walk'd in,
  Said Hob, that must have been the way.
 Hob vanish'd---Mrs. Stitch soon after,
 Furnish'd another scene for laughter;
 She jogg'd her Spouse, and whisper'd low,
 Is Robin up and gone, or no?
 Bodkin reply'd, at break of day,
 Two hours ago he stole away:
I dreamt, said she, and then awoke,
  I thought 'twas you in such a cue,
  I doubted whether it was you;
I thought you drove away like smoak:
  I never felt so much delight,
  Either in sleeping or awake,
  I was afraid 'twas some mistake;
What would I give to dream it every night!
  I was surpriz'd to find you grown
  So lusty, and with so much bone,

        And

And twice as ftrong, and ftronger too,
    Than when upon our wedding fheets,
For all that I could fay or do ;
    You robb'd me of my virgin fweets.
'Twas but a dream, faid Stitch, that's plain,
I'll try to make you dream again ;
He did his beft, and Morpheus feiz'd her foon,
Bodkin got up at nine, fhe flept till noon.---

M O R A L

The fex, faid a phyfician of the college,
    Like men, are either faints or finners,
Like Eve, they long fo much for knowledge,
    They fcarce have time to eat their dinners.
The difference between them and us,
    Is this, the fex, both great and fmall,
All look as innocent as pufs,
    The greateft hypocrite of all.
But men oft glory in their fhame,
And take our wives for lawful game.
Put not your truft in leather breeches,
    Whether your wife's behind you, or before,
They all can tell, they are fuch witches,
    Whether you fleep, or only feign a fnore.

She

She knows her time, fhe gives an intimation,
 To Galligafkins, and if he's inclin'd,
He will accept of Madam's invitation,
 Juft as it fuits, before you or behind.

THE DAINTY WIDOW'S TALE.

T A L E   VI.

MY Tale is every bit a Moral,
 A hint for delicate complexions,
Black, brown, and fair, or red as coral,
 May benefit by my reflexions.
In artifice, moft of us deal,
 And ladies that affect fine feelings,
Mean to declare, how fine they feel,
 All over in their tender dealings.
Reach me that peach, faid I, my dear,
 It fets my teeth on edge faid Prue,
It makes me feel all over queer,
 Has it not that effect on you ?

Your

Your teeth on edge, my dear! I underftand,
 I would not give the creature any quarter,
When you have got Eve's fruit into your hand,
 Mifs, I fuppofe, faid I, your mouth muft water.
Prue redden'd, not from fhame, but fpite,
I fee, faid I, my guefs is right.

THE BARONESS'S TALE.

T A L E   VII.

A Merry ftory's better far,
 Than a lampoon or witty libel:
Mine is from Margaret of Navarre,
 As true as any in the bible.
Vrai comme l'Evangile, 'tis c'en,
 True as the gofpel, fays the queen.
Three Merchants of Savoy, I know not when,
 Were travelling, each with his fpoufe,
Pilgrims to Saint Antonio of Vienne,
 All of them bound by previous vows,

In

In journeying to live together,
    Not like their fathers and their mothers,
    But like three fifters, and three brothers,
  As well in cold as in hot weather.
    Like them in beds apart to lie,
    In chambers feperate, but nigh.
Leaft through miftake, fifter and brother,
    Or in their fleep or in the dark,
Might tumble one upon another,
    And the collifion ftrike a fpark.
Which meeting with the tinder box,
    Is all that they require;
All fuch combuftibles as fmocks,
    To make the leaft inflammable catch fire.
They were all left in full poffeffion,
    Of every other fenfe, or tafte,
That is to ufe them with difcretion,
    You know there's none, below the waift.
At Chambery arriving, our three pair,
    Spared no expence at their hotel,
Excellent wine and plenty of good fare,
    All appetites but one, fared well.
They fupp'd, and feem'd fo loath to part;
    The brothers, and the fifters both,
I am perfuaded from my heart,
    Had much ado to keep their oath.

The

The ladies to their room repair'd,
   To chat both in and out of bed,
Their beds before had been prepar'd,
   Three, with one pillow, for each head.
  But were their hufbands there, *and thereabout*,
      Inftead of one,
      Had there been none,
  I do believe *they could have done without*.
I need not tell you, when three Dames,
   Gather'd together are undreffing,
They call things by their naked names,
   So plain, they leave no room for gueffing:
When the difcourfe is turn'd from fafhions,
To certain objects of the paffions;
And in undreffing you may fwear,
They fhew their charms, and they compare.———
Three Monks, all three Father Confeffors,
   That lay hard by, wonder'd to hear,
The ladies talking like profeffors,
   In terms of art diftinct and clear:
which made the holy fathers *rife*,
And ftand and liften with furprife,
Then gliding to the door they fpy'd,
   Up, on their beds, all in their fhifts,
The three fair Dames that fcorn'd to hide,
   Any of God's bounteous gifts.

H

The Monks, much edify'd retir'd,
　And by Saint Francis were infpir'd.
They knew they lay without a mate ;
　　And like brave foldiers of Saint Francis,
Refolv'd they fhould no longer wait,
　　And fuffer for their hufbands fancies.
Saint Francis muft have been their guide ;
　　Moft certainly Saint Francis knew,
The ladies after the review---
　　Forgot the key was left on the outfide.
Now filence reign'd, the fair ones flept,
　　And out the watchful brethren came,
Secur'd the door, and foftly crept,
　　Each bold Francifcan to his flame.
There was no time for them to fpare,
　　For preface or folicitation,
They feiz'd Time by the lock of hair,
　　Without one word on the occafion.
Finding their dears fo hot and greedy,
　　And fo foon up and on again.;
The ladies, who were alfo needy,
　　Found that refiftance would be vain.
One of the fifters had a notion,
　　The alteration was fo ftrange,
That hers had taken fome love potion,
　　To make fo very great a change.

They bore it all with patient bearing,
    And without uttering a word :
All the three wives, whilft they were pairing,
    Thought theirs the only pairing bird.
  Each held her tongue, and took her feed,
  Pitying the two that ftood in need.
The Champions, after their great deeds,
    Gently retir'd, exhaufted quite ;
And, with their baggage and their beads,
    March'd off as foon as it was light.
The Merchants flept fo long, thanks to the wine,
    So well to both the parties fuited,
Their heads, on waking, ach'd no more than mine,
    And their wives rofe, frefh and recruited.
Then huddling on their clothes, in the meanwhile
    Their tongues perpetually wagging,
The fmarteft cried, with an arch fmile,
    And with a tone of voice like bragging,
Pray, were you wak'd, like me, laft night ?
    Had you a vifit from your Spoufes ?——
If yours were in as fine a plight,
    They muft have been about your houfes——
Mine wak'd me, and away he fcour'd
    At once, and ran me out of breath ;
I thought I fhould have been devour'd ;
    Prefs'd, bulgg'd, and fqueez'd, and crufh'd to death.

Ours

Ours too were in as good condition,

 The others faid——What could it mean?

It muſt have been the prohibition,

 They all agreed, that made them all ſo keen.

 Undoubtedly, faid Madam Smart;

 Oft have I wonder'd, for my part,

With what indifference they begin,

 And jog on in a lawful deed;

But let it be a mortal ſin,

 Heaven's, with what ardour they proceed!——

The men were up, and in their jackets,

 And were juſt putting on their ſhoes,

When their wives enter'd with their packets,

 Full of glad tidings and great news.

No wonder that you lay.till noon,

 After your laſt night's feats, faid they,

To come and break your oaths ſo ſoon,

 And make us break ours too, was not fair play.

Each to her Huſband then repeated,

 How ſuddenly ſhe was ſurpris'd,

How handſomely ſhe had been treated,

 For which ſhe hop'd he would not be chaſtis'd.

'The fault was his, ſhe had no blame;

   She was ſo hurry'd,

   Bated and worry'd,

If 'twas to do again, ſhe would do the ſame.——

          You

You muft be drunk or mad, I fear,
    The hufband cried, 'tis a clear cafe,
I never ftir'd, or I'm not here,
    Out of my bed, out of this place;
    And fo they one and all declared,
    And look'd like fimpletons and ftared.
The women blufh'd up to the ears,
    Firft thought of this, and then of that,
And their fufpicions and their fears,
    Made them begin to fmell a rat.
A Merchant, wifer than the reft,
    Making a fign they underftood,
Laugh'd and faid, wife, we were in jeft,
    My fins I hope have done us good.
I hope, faid he, you'll wifh me joy,
    And our endeavours and joint labours,
Will be productive of a boy,
    I wifh the fame, for my two neighbours.
An act, faid he, you will allow,
        Of fo great merit,
It muft repair our broken vow,
    You know, we broke it with great fpirit.
'Twas not enough, faid Miftrefs Sly,
    To break your oath, but you muft run,
And go to bed to make a lye,
    For which you don't deferve a fon;

I

And

And yet I hope and expect rather,
Your son will not be like his father;
With that the females in a titter,
Retir'd to gather up the litter.
The women gone, the Merchant cry'd,
Brothers, you fee how matters go,
Our ladies have been Monkcupy'd,
Which is not fit for them to know;
We muſt lock up this fecret in our trunks,
For if the faithful partners of our beds
Should know their obligations to the Monks,
Monks will be always running in their heads.
To pocket the affront is right,
As to our wives 'tis beſt you'll own,
To lie with them ourfelves at night,
And never let them lie alone;
Whether the ladies doubts were clear'd away,
I never heard fo cannot fay;
But I have heard that ever after,
Whene'er they met at any place,
And look'd each other in the face,
They fell into a fit of laughter.
And with great gratitude and reafon,
For their devotion in due feafon,

His

His blefling Saint Antonio fent,
   With three huge boys, made and conceiv'd,
   Monaftically, 'tis believ'd,
To the fix pilgrims great content.——

M O R A L.

Cleave to your wives, the fcripture fays,
   I fay, that cleaving is a blefling,
But you muft ftick and cleave always,
   Or elfe your head may get a drefling.
As clofe, as if you were tied and buckled,
   So clofe no creature can get at her ;
You might my Lord, be made a cuckold,
   And I know nothing of the matter.
To make a vow to leave your wife in danger,
   And let her lie alone and fob her,
Is to lock up your cafh, before a ftranger,
   And tempt him to become a robber ;
   Which was exemplified you find,
   In three bold Monks, all of one mind——
This truth will follow from that fequel,
   Which ought to be obferv'd and known,
   That one of us left quite alone,
Or three of us together, are things equal.

T H E

THE LAWYER'S TALE.

TALE VIII.

MY ſtory's true, as well as new,
  Of folks I know, that ſhall be namelefs,
Their real names are nought to you,
  I'll call my knight, Sir Joſeph Shamelefs.
His lady's woman, Kitty Patience,
  With wicked eyes, her teeth two rows of pearl,
  And all the ſequel of the girl,
A complication of temptations.
The knight had now and then the gout,
  To have it only now and then,
  Is of great uſe to many men,
It has its merits without doubt.
Amongſt the proverbs of my ſire,
  The gout I have often heard him call,
The potent parent of deſire,
  Without whoſe aid his doings were but ſmall——
 I mean he was not half ſo ſtout,
 And ſometimes could not make it out
  ————————— At all.

My

My Lady in her ftays, and Kitty lacing;
  My Lady's fingers bufy round the border,
Giving her fnowy breafts a proper bracing,
  To keep them at a diftance, and in order:
  So proud and bold they ftand when they are parted,
  When they are near they droop, and look faint-hearted.
The Knight came in——Said he, how finely
  You plump them out, they look divinely——
Kitty's tetons have got no ftay,
  They feem to fcorn any affiftance;
If they fhould happen to give way,
  They'll turn again, and make refiftance:
With that, he thrufts his hand into her neck;
  My Lady turn'd about and fmil'd,
Without the leaft rebuke or check,
  She only faid, you fhould not let him, child,
  Patience reply'd, with downcaft eye,
  I thought there was no harm, as you were by——
My Lady faid, no, not the leaft——
  Kitty, I have feen you quite undreft;
If you will treat him with a feaft,
  Thefe two are vouchers for the reft.
Kitty was then miftrefs of arts;
  The Knight, without a cry of murther,
Long fince had vifited thofe parts,
  And gone till he could go no further.

            K

                                       His

His Lady knew that he lov'd change ;

    He knew her paffions were as ftrong,

She could not be averfe to range,

    She was fo apt to fancy things and long.

They went and came without each other's knowing,

    Both of them lov'd to change the fcene ;

They never afk'd where they were going,

    Nor once enquir'd where each had been——

One day the Knight fell faft afleep,

    The Knight was in his gouty chair ;

A Captain and my Lady fair,

    On the fettee in meditation deep.

She rofe and went behind the fcreen,

And he to fee what fhe could mean.

They ftay'd not there you muft have thought,

Standing like fools and doing nought.

At the conclufion of their fport,

    And whilft the room and fcreen were fhaking ;

Sir Jofeph heard her breathing fhort,

    Juft at the moment he was waking.

He was acquainted with her notes,

    And knew, that from her dying fong,

    Her time was come, 'twould not be long

Before fhe fhook her petticoats :

    Her petticoats to fmooth the gathers,

    Juft like a hen, that fhakes her feathers---

As

As long as he could hear them prancing
He would not interrupt their dancing.
What noife was that? Sir Joſeph cried ;
    'Twas a ſtrange noiſe I heard juſt now,
My lady readily replied,
    I can't account for it I vow ;
For God's ſake let us run away,
It was an earthquake I dare ſay :
An a-ſe quake, ſaid the Knight, it was a ſquall !
A ſudden guſt of wind, that's all---
And ſo ſhe ſaid the Captain ſaid before :
The Captain's in the right, Sir Joſeph ſwore.---
They took their evening walk, ſhe and her friend,
    Kitty came down to make Sir James's tea,
The Knight told Kitty in the end,
    What he had heard, but could not ſtir to ſee.
If you can catch them in the fact,
    And can but ſee what I heard now,
With proofs enough to get an Act,
    Who knows but I may marry you?
Kitty you ſhall not lie alone,
I'll either marry you or none.
Patience, whoſe name implies ſubmiſſion,
Soon executed her commiſſion,
Kitty's was ocular demonſtration ;
    The Captain ſitting like a lout,

Her

Her Lady in a fituation,
    As if the Captain had the gout.
Said he, do fhew me how fhe did it ;
    She anfwer'd modeftly, I'll try ;
And then fhe dandled it and flid it,
    And Kitty did it by and by.
'Twas the firft time fhe play'd upon the ftage,
    But afterwards few could play better,
In any part fhe could engage,
    The ableft Manager could fet her.
So far from bold, Kitty 'till then,
    Was fo difcreet, you could not guefs ;
Efpecially amongft the men,
    Which were more modeft, Kitty's looks or drefs.
But now fhe foon threw off the mafk,
    She gave herfelf prodigious airs,
You may be fure, you need not afk,
    As well above, as below ftairs.
There was a Lawyer, that liv'd near,
    For whom at laft, Sir Jofeph fent,
And order'd Kitty to appear,
    Having told the Lawyer his intent.
Patience, faid he, it is no fhame,
    Be not afham'd to fpeak the truth,
You muft defcribe the romping game,
    My Lady, romping with the youth.

                              Kittty

Kitty look'd down, put on a frown,

    Look'd up, and then fhe look'd afide ;

She pull'd a pin out of her gown,

    Look'd at the pin, and then reply'd——

I faw my Lady with her legs aftride,

    Wagging her tail' upon the Captain's knee ;

And after fhe had done her ride,

    Sit like a bird perch'd on a tree :

Upon her perch fhe did not long remain,

    He gave a fpring, and fhe fet out again.

I never could have thought of fuch a trick——

    I faw it through my Lady's clofet door :

The very fight made me fo fick,

    I could not ftay to fee it any more ;

But ran directly from the place,

    And went into the open air,

And after told his Honour the whole cafe ;

    Sitting exactly then, as he fits there.

Altho' the gout had left his feet,

    Tell it again, he faid, and bring a feat.

I knew Sir Jofeph's meaning, I dare fay ;

    Sir Jofeph thought that I would vary,

    In my relating her vagary ;

He knows I always told it the fame way,

    For he has made me tell it o'er and o'er,

    A dozen times at leaft, if not a fcore——

L

Did you fee *rem in re?* faid he——
   I did, faid fhe; firft, on dry land,
   I faw *rem* in my Lady's hand;
And after that, faw *rem in re.*

She put it there; I faw how it was teas'd——
   Now it was quite up to the chin,
   And then again half out half in,
   Juft as my Lady pleas'd.

Her ftays and petticoats upon the floor,
She in her fhift and gown, with nothing more;
And all the time her fhift and gown,
   Up to her fhoulders like a fhawl,
As fhe went up and down
   I faw it all.——

The Lawyer faid, were you alone?
Was there none elfe?——Said fhe, not one.——
One witnefs, Madam, will not do.
Why, Mifs, faid he, were there not two?
   And as Sir Jofeph fent you out——
   He told me fo;
   Why would you go
   Alone to fcout?——

I had a cafe the other night——
   Exactly the fame cafe, as it was ftated,
Between a Damfel and a Knight,
   But not by far fo well related.

The

The evidence is not deficient,
For there are three, two are fufficient.
And therefore I advife, Mifs Kitty,
 To leave off fpying; I know fpies
 That talk and fee, altho' their eyes
Are not fo fine, nor teeth fo pretty:
 And females, that are as difcerning,
 But very fhort of Mifs in learning.——
Upon fome hints thrown out by Patience,
 Before my Lady, fhe from thence,
Set maids to watch, made preparations,
 And got enough for her defence.
Before the Lawyer's wife they came,
 With all the facts, clearly defcrib'd and well;
They could not have told him for fhame,
 All that fhe undertook to tell.]
Sir Jofeph faid, Kitty, you fee
 A fpy is but a forry trade;
 I found, I thought, one cunning jade,
I find my Lady has found three.
 And therefore we muft be content,
 And lie together with my wife's confent:
She will not care with whom I'm fleeping,
 Provided both are bound and ty'd,
That information got by peeping,
 Shall not avail on either fide.

So

So both remain, coupled per force,
    'Till Death has got her in his power,
    Or she's entitled to her dower,
Neither can suffer a divorce.

M O R A L

There are not more than six or seven,
    I think, at farthest, in a year,
Of weddings that are made in Heaven,
    All other weddings are made here.
   At concerts, balls, at fairs and races,
   Scarb'rough and all terraqueous places.
Suppose you have no friend above,
    And it should chance to be your fate,
Instead of a celestial dove,
    To get a wild-goose for your mate.
E'en let her take her flight and roam,
    Never let that disturb your rest,
Provide a substitute at home,
    Of a bad bargain make the best :
   The best you can, I ought to say ;
   The best is——putting her away.

THE

THE BARON'S TALE.

TALE IX.

LADIES, faid Frank, with ladies walking,
    Pleafe to obferve that aviary there,
Suppofe their finging goes for talking,
    Their down, for any downy hair.
They are the types of our gay world,
    You know fine feathers make fine birds,
Our belles like theirs painted and curl'd
    With crimfon cheeks, and breafts like curds.
  Our macaronies with their muffs,
    Are not like finging birds, but piping ruffs.
The only difference I find,
    Our beaux are vain, the ruffs are proud,
All our belles feign, theirs fpeak their mind,
    But are as talkative and loud.
  Pray ladies walk a little nearer,
    You'll fee the microcofm clearer ;
Behold thofe lovers fitting cooing,
    With little interludes of billing,
Others proceeding without wooing ;
    Both are fo amorous and willing ;

Theirs

Their hops, love-feasts and agapees;
  Our balls, methodist night-wakes, cotteries;
That bird in dishabille alone,
    Is a fine lady in the pout,
'Till her fine feathers are full grown
    Her ladyship frequents no rout.——
Said Lady Bridget your remarks are smart,
    But where are there old maids I pray?
With your sharp eyes and all your art,
    Can you defcry one bachelor grown grey?
    Faith, Frank reply'd, 'twould be the fame thing here,
    Could we contract, like them, from year to year.
    Maids can contract on credit now,
    She faid, but not with folks like you.
Marry, and for your fins atone,
    A wife is eafy to befpeak,
Tho' you are not a precious ftone,
    She'll take you for a verd antique.
    My fins might have been pardon'd long ago, .
    I could, faid Frank, have married you, you know.
    At thirty, one may venture on a wife,
    At forty-eight, I dare not for my life.
Liften, and I will tell you why
    At forty there is fo much danger;
Ladies a ftory hangs thereby,
    None of you ever heard a ftranger,

In

In Lombard-ftreet there dwelt a Banker,
 Not quite a hundred years ago ;
At thirty-nine he dropp'd his anchor,
 About the purlieu's of Soho.
Service of plate, pinery, villa ;
 Yet God forgive him for his pride ;
And with a Venus for his pillow,
 This Banker was not fatisfy'd.
In Parliament he had a feat,
 But by deep ftudy and reflexion,
And by converfing with the great,
 He found the want of a connexion :
That honour feldom is conferr'd,
 On people of our rank and ftation,
Unlefs it cannot be deferr'd,
 It requires great confideration.
At laft, a Peer offer'd his niece,
 That had been offer'd to a pleader,
A fine plump, buxom, roomy piece,
 Calculated for a breeder.
Mifs and her Lover fcarce were feated——
 At once fhe yielded to the Banker ;
His errand was not twice repeated,
 Before he rofe to kifs and thank her.
 This alfo is the ton at prefent,
 And more compendious and pleafant.

Upon

Upon the wedding-night, in fum,
Having arriv'd at kingdom come;
  Attack'd the fort with his whole power,
   Forc'd barricades, gates, and portcullis,
   With its appendant chains and pullies,
  He broke into the dungeon tower:
But when he thought his victory compleat,
A fudden fally forc'd him to retreat——
You never read of fuch a Knight,
  In any chronicle before,
A little boy put him to flight,
  And drove him from the dungeon door:
Screaming aloud, as the Knight fled,
Behold the bride was brought to bed!
Hearing the fhout, the Bridemaids blufh'd;
  One man cried, girls, the caftle's won,
Such an affair muft not be hufh'd,
  But the Bride's part feems overdone.
Why fcream and fhriek, 'twas not like taking Troy?
Up with the poffet, let us wifh them joy.
They ran up ftairs; then rapp'd and cry'd,
Refrefhment for the Groom and Bride!
  After fo hardy an adventure!
   No anfwer came; the Bridgroom rofe,
   And leifurely put on his cloaths,
  Sat by the fire and bad them enter.

           Our

Our Bridemaids thought the place was ta'en,
  That both the citadel and town,
  Were laid in afhes, or pull'd down,
They heard the fhrieks and cries fo plain:
  At prefent, they have chang'd their mind,
  Said one, or elfe they muft be blind.
For far from a triumphant form,
  His downcaft eyes and drooping creft,
Pronounce it a defective ftorm,
  Or a drawn battle at the beft.
The Bridegroom cried, the caufe lies yonder,
A caufe to ruminate and ponder ;
'Twould make the richeft Nabob ftare,
Such an expence he could not bear ;
Hardly the king, much lefs a peer ;
  If every time fhe takes a bout,
  A Mafter or a Mifs pops out,
What muft they mount to in a year ?
  On which he unclos'd the curtains where fhe laid,
  Somewhat abafh'd, but not difmay'd.
He turn'd the cloaths down, and fubjoin'd,
  'Tis worth your while to fee what's in't,
Ecce Homo ! Stamp'd and coin'd,
  An hour ago, frefh from the mint ;
  Then made his bow, and march'd off fmiling,
  Without reproaching, or reviling.

N

In

In ten days after, fhe and her homuncle,

Return'd to their right honourable uncle.

He knew, before he took her to Soho,

    The whole houfe knew it by the bye,

She had not many weeks to go,

    But did not think her time fo nigh.

A Privy Council then was fitting,

    In Cloacina's temple met,

Of females arguing and fh———,

    About a certain famous bet.

What fhare my Lord had in the cow and calf,

    Whether the whole or only half?

The fentence, without an appeal,

    Wrote on the wall, feal'd with the Privy Seal.

The fentence written there, was droll,

    The calf fhould not be cut in two,

The Butler fhould enjoy it whole,

    His Lordfhip might divide the cow,

And Lord have mercy on her foul.

Said, Lady Bridget, great or fmall,

    There is fome rifk, I do confefs,

    At forty, nay, perhaps at lefs;

Marry before, or not at all:

Which

Which for a moral, may fuffice,
For any Bachelor that's wife.——

N O T E.

A Lady upon her wedding night was brought to-bed, in the Cent Nouvelles
Nouvelles——the Tale is taken from this hint——the hint, and very little more
befide.

THE PHYSICIAN'S TALE.

T A L E   X.

AMONGST the Cent Nouvelles Nouvelles,
　　Some Tales unmodernis'd remain,
Which I would not attempt to tell,
　　Had they been told by La Fontaine ;
And this of mine amongft the reft,
　　Call'd Antidote de la Pefte.
Said Mrs. Slip Slop that may be,
　　But of all ftories I *admier*,
　　Hans Carvel told by Matthew Prior,
No one can tell a tale like *he.*

Carvel,

Carvel, impotent and old,
　　His finger in his wife's gold ring;
How do you know that it was gold?
　　The Doctor *Or* said, '*twas no such thing.*
Carvel's wife's picture, I declare,
　　Is always drawn with auburn hair :
Like Mrs. Slip Slop's, lock for lock;
　　Bushy, and curling very fine,
　　Just like the tendrils of a vine,
About a stake or stumpy stock.
Doctor proceed in your own way,
　　My Lady cry'd; Slip Slop have done,
You talk and know not what you say,
　　When once your tongue begins to run.
In Dauphiny, by his relation,
　　A plague arose that rag'd as sore,
And caus'd as great a desolation,
　　As that of Athens heretofore.
When once the plague is upon duty,
　　To punish mortals for their sins,
It neither cares for youth nor beauty,
　　For high, nor low, for outs nor ins——
Upon a sweet young lady's face,
　　It breath'd its pestilential breath,
The fair one would not quit the place,
　　Neither for the plague nor death.

In

In cities ftorm'd, 'twere better far,
   Whate'er betide,
   For a young maiden to abide,
And take the accidents of war.
Struck on a fudden and difmay'd,
   To a good widow fhe repair'd,
Who neither was herfelf afraid,
   Nor for her lovely friend defpair'd;
But gave her cordials, and in brief,
Hope, the beft cordial for grief.
This is no feafon for difguife;
   Have you, faid fhe, eat of the Tree of Life,
That makes us at fifteen as wife,
   As a fage dowager or wife.
The poor thing cry'd, oh! if I had,
I fhould not think my fate fo fad!
Many die young, and in full bloom,
But few like me go to their tomb.
Not one, if we could know the truth,
   When Love in every artery beats,
With all the powers and charms of youth,
   Without once tafting of its fweets.
Even now, Death would not be fo frightful,
   If I could get before I go,
   A hearty meal of what you know,
And what I am told, is fo delightful——

And if God pleafe;

  May be a cure for the difeafe.

Her friend reply'd, that is foon done;

    For, God be thank'd, there are enow,

    Enow, that have nought elfe to do;

The fair maid cry'd, for God's fake run:

  I know at leaft of three or four,

  That I have oft' refus'd before;

One very much againft my will:

    'Tis mafter John, bring him anon,

    For by St. Luke, my mafter John,

Muft either cure or kill.

  Behold him ready at her beck,

  Behold her arms about his neck;

At once, *pour vous le couper court*,

    There was no *petite oye*, no toys,

    Like half fledg'd girls and foolifh boys,.

To anticede *parfait amour*.

    Finifh'd, repeated o'er and o'er,

    'Till mafter John could do no more..

    She ftay'd and play'd, not without pain,

    But found it all labour in vain:

My dear, faid fhe, you have done me good;

  I thank you for your good intention,

But yet you cannot cool my blood,

  With all your goodnefs and attention.

Go

Go, my dear love, and go to bed,
  And fend the Marquis in your ftead.
He fent the Marquis, then laid down,
  Sent for the Curate and confefs'd ;
And after that obtain'd the crown
  Of martyrdom amongft the blefs'd.——
  The Marquis far'd the very fame,
  And dy'd without quenching her flame.
The Widow recommended next,
  A fubject for the vacant chair,
A fwain that never was perplex'd,
  Either with thinking or with care ;
Form'd and conftructed on a plan,
  To build a compleat Widow's man ;
During the whole co-operation,
  Far more fevere than I can paint,
'Till he was forc'd to quit his ftation,
  She never utter'd a complaint.
He went home jaded you'll believe ;
  But how, without St. Luke's protection,
  He fhould efcape without infection,
Is not fo eafy to conceive.
Her father hearing fhe was fmitten,
  Sent a fedan and chairmen able,
To bring her home as was befitting,
  But firft to land her in the ftable,

'Till

'Till they were ready to receive her,

    And all things got that could relieve her.

As frefh as when fhe firft fet out,

    Before fhe went to the peft-room,

She took a handfome farewell bout,

    Concluding with her Father's Groom.

The Damfel, when her bed was ready,

    Leaning upon her Nurfe, retir'd,

Refign'd and fteady ;

    And four hours after the poor Groom expir'd.

Confign'd to her old Nurfe's care,

    She had not lain above two hours,

    Before the fweat broke out in fhowers,

Next came on each fide, you know where,

    A *bijoux* very fine to fee,

    This like her watch, and that like her etwi :

    Then fell into a fleep profound,

    And wak'd next morning fafe and found.

Three months were paft, the fact was clear,

    She prov'd with child, nor would deny it——

To her good Mother, as you'll hear,

    She own'd, in part, how fhe came by it.——

Three of the candidates were gone,

    Three fhe deftroy'd you know before,

    Three out of four,

    Therefore it fell to the furviving one ;

                     On

On whom fhe was beftow'd in marriage;
    And put an end to all difpute,
    About the planter and the fruit,
Next day by a mifcarriage.———

THE DOCTOR'S ADVICE.

Nature has taken fpecial care,
    If you confider and examine,
To guard the fair,
    Againft plague, peftilence and famine.
Therefore we ought to give God praife,
    That they're not fcarce, but in great plenty,
    Or otherwife, for fuch a dainty,
We fhould be cutting throats always.
For our fakes, Ladies, and your own,
    If there fhould happen to appear,
    The Influenza, like laft year,
Follow this regimen alone.
As to the dofe, I cannot guefs,
    Unlefs I knew your conftitution,
It may be more, it may be lefs,
    But more or lefs, take it with refolution.———
    This you muft note,
A plague requires, much more than a fore throat.

P

THE

THE APOTHECARY'S TALE.

TALE XI.

APOTHECARIES are not fit,
   None but Apothecary King,
To deal in gallantry or wit,
      They may tell tales, or ditties fing.
   Always providing and fuppofing,
      They are not of their own compofing;
   As I am call'd on in fucceffion,
   I fhall ftick clofe to my profeffion.
A Quack, in a fmall country town,
      According to report,
Got great renown,
      For his great cures of every fort.
   He never ufed to bleed or blifter,
      Or to give bolus pill or potion,
      His panacea was a lotion,
   Or a detergent, call'd a clyfter;

                                              And

And this was conftantly apply'd,
    Upon the fpot where he refided,
To every backfide
    That would abide it.
A Cobler came from a great diftance,
    With a full confidence poffefs'd,
Imploring his affiftance,
    Taking him for a conjuror profefs'd.
For he had heard in various places,
    Of his fuccefs in conjuring cafes.
Befide his ftall and cobling gift,
    He kept a ftye,
And therein kept a boar whereby,
    He made a tolerable fhift.
An ancient pig, of that fair fex,
    Came on a vifit to the boar,
The boar was gone, which needs muft vex,
    And make the matron gruntle fore.
The Cobler's truft was in the cunning man,
    He fearch'd woods, vallies, hills and plains,
    But all in vain, for all his pains ;
So to the conjuror he ran.
The Ladies ought to know before
    Your Tale goes on, faid the Phyfician,
The definition of a boar——
    'Tis Mrs. Slip Slop's definition——

                                       An

An animal with a curl'd tail,

    With *teſtibles* like melons more than figs,

The moſt continuaceous male,

    Ingeniouſly contrived for making pigs :

    Pigs, made between ſleeping and waking,

    They take ſo long a time in making.

    From whence, by Mrs. Slip Slop's leave,

      To make the matter ſtill more plain, ·

      A metaphor is ta'en,

    That from her drawing you'll conceive.

    Thus, all the maccaroni corps,

      Call a long ſtory, or narration,

    Which is a ſlow dull operation,

        A boar.

You underſtand it now, thanks to your veſtal ;

    And, my dear Ladies, I implore you,

Hark to the Knight of the *great* Peſtle,

    I promiſe you, he will not boar you.

    The Cobler ſqueezing through the crowd,

      The Doctor heard him aſk his aid,

      But could make nought of what he ſaid,

    The Doctor's patients talked ſo loud.

Take him away, the Doctor cried,

    Convey him quickly to the artiſt,

Let him immediately be plied

    With an injection of the ſmarteſt.

On

On which they took him as directed,
   And all at once, not by degrees,
Crispin was copioufly injected,
    Then fet at large, paying his fees.

As he march'd home, he made a ftop,
  The remedy began to work ;
Which forc'd the Cobler to uncork,
  A dunghill drank it every drop :
Like bachelors and black-legg'd gamblers ;
Boars run about and are great ramblers.

  Our Cobler's boar was lodging there,
     And grunting at the noife, put out his fnout,
    On which the Cobler turn'd about,
  Held up his hands, and utter'd a fhort prayer.
The Lord be prais'd, faid he and for the fame,
Laudamus to the Conjuror's name.
Not only he, his wife, his fifter,
   The Parifh and the Vicar too,
Believe it was the Doctor's clyfter,
    That found his pig out, what think you ?

Q.   MORAL.

MORAL

In times of troubles and of war,
    A Conjuror's no bad vocation,
Better by far,
    Than in a quiet fituation.
The country vulgar always run,
    To the Attorney, Parfon, Squire,
    Or London Rider to enquire,
Whether or no they are undone :
    And we that think ourfelves their betters,
    Apply to fome great man of letters :
To Doctor Johnfon, not the amphibious ;
    To Doctor Prieftley, Franklin's rival;
Or to the reverend and ambiguous
        Mr. Wy——l;
Who fend us to fome cunning man,
    To Fox or Burke,
    Or my Lord Smirk,
The cunningeft of all the clan.
Thefe mount the therapeutick roftrum,
    One deals in amulets and charms,
Another fells a famous noftrum,
    That animates, corrects and warms ;
The third, a fubtile diftillation
To numb the fenfe of *amputation.*

If

If any of them fhould by chance,
   Guefs right, and make a lucky hit,
Mercy upon us ! how they prance !
   How we fing praifes and are bit.

N O T E.

This Tale in part is taken from the Cent Nouvelles Nouvelles; it is not every one that can read them ; if the reader can, he is defired to compare with thofe, the Tales that are in fome meafure borrowed from thence, and which are always mentioned ; and he will obferve, that the author, is neither a tranflator, nor an imitator; but has an indifputable right, with Fontaine, to originality. The Lady is too modeft to have made the requeft herfelf, it is made at the requeft of the publifher.

F I N I S.

www.ingramcontent.com/pod-product-compliance
Lightning Source LLC
Chambersburg PA
CBHW022154020726
47496CB00008B/2717